After reading *The Decameron* _____ccio, in which the threat of disease affects how a group of ten people spend their last few days, I thought about how these characters might be different in a modern context. This modern context is partially influenced by misinformation and 'fake news', particularly its ability to shape religious belief. As a result, I decided to set the novel in an isolated, impressionable community – one that could potentially be anywhere – to show that the growth of religious extremism and its effects on people is easily possible at any time, given the right circumstances. This novel delves into the feelings of different community members as they struggle to cope with the consequences that viral disease under cultish leadership has brought to Greenville.

The
Ascension
of Greenville

The
Ascension
of Greenville

A N N A   P A T T L E

BROWN
DOG
BOOKS

Published under licence by Brown Dog Books and
The Self-Publishing Partnership, 7 Green Park Station, Bath BA1 1JB

www.selfpublishingpartnership.co.uk

ISBN printed book: 978-1-83952-264-2
ISBN e-book: 978-1-83952-265-9

Cover design by Kevin Rylands
Internal design by Andrew Easton

Printed and bound in the UK

This book is printed on FSC certified paper

In memory of the struggles endured by many during the COVID-19 pandemic, which allowed me to reflect on the impacts a virus can have on a community.

CHAPTER 1

HONESTY

The weighty sound of the words from my throat was intoxicating. They seemed to coat the heads of the church attendees in a silver layer, like a cloud of exhaled cigar smoke that teased their senses as it danced and swirled in unpredictable swells. It was winter and even with everyone in the town gathered together, warming the building with their movement, my breath still stained the air in cold puffs. I paused to take a sip of icy water from the cup resting on the pulpit stand and watched as dozens of eyes followed my movement. How strangely euphoric.

Down in the first row of seating I saw the group of children that I had been mentoring yesterday. The more I became aware of the weight of their round eyes on me, the more I felt my gravity. How light I felt in that moment! How effortlessly divine I must have appeared to them, with my polished white robes and solemn black beads around my neck. Would I be their deity? Their irrefutable voice of authority? I spread my arms out wide and continued.

'The incubation period of the virus varies from person to person. For some, the symptoms can hold off for months. Years. For others, it is simply a matter of days.' I cracked a smile. 'Don't forget to eat your vegetables and keep your immune system strong. We can't have one of you dropping dead because you forgot to finish your carrots at dinner.'

Too light? A seething frustration in my gut as I heard only a few scattered laughs. A little more emphasis on the 'forgot to finish' next time. Maybe some stress on 'car-rots'.

'However, from the trends that have been detected by scientists, once you catch the virus, there doesn't seem to be much that modern medicine can do. We haven't the ability to treat anyone, and since this virus is so contagious and so extreme in its nature, our best hope is to prevent it from reaching Greenville altogether. Thankfully, Utah isn't largely populated like New York, Los Angeles and the like, so if we follow the guidelines and keep hope in our hearts, we're sure to be fine.' I smiled warmly, ignoring the pallid expressions below the pulpit.

The beating heart of the crowd murmured nervously. People were skittish, I realised. I shouldn't have joked about carrots; jokes at a time like this didn't help with relatability, only portrayed me as distanced and aloof from the gravity of the situation. I gave my best smile once more. A smile of comfort, I instructed myself. Nothing but a shepherd encouraging his sheep into their pens. I tugged my mouth to the sides and I felt a slight shift in the crowd, a spreading outwards and an opening up. It was being received well, then. How pleasing to know that such a smile could change the atmosphere of a room. I needed to think of a name for myself. What was a divine-like name? 'Zeus' would stretch my ego too much, and 'Ares' was too violent. I supposed I would stick with 'Doctor Harrison', although I resented the unromantic, mundane sound of it. History textbooks would probably paint me as a plain, middle-aged man with a round belly and beady eyes. I saw none of those things when I looked in the mirror, but I knew how perception could be distorted with time. Could my handsome cheekbones and sun-lit eyes not negate the impression that 'Harrison' gave? I wondered what size my picture would be on the page. Whether it would be colourised or black and white.

I smiled again, this time a private smile.

I was almost reeling, head slowly tipping backwards as I anticipated the exhilaration of my future worldwide renown. The Septosect would finally gain recognition, and my name would be in print right next to it. The Lord was going to be so proud.

A pair of eyes were staring hard at my mouth. I glanced downwards. One of the children from yesterday, Halle. She frowned at me, and I realised I had forgotten to turn away before I let my face express private emotions. I would have to watch her closely; children of that age were always more observant than one gave them credit for. I waited until the church had quietened down once more.

'From the time that you catch the virus, you cannot pass it on unless you are showing symptoms. Symptoms include rapid sneezing, shallow breath and reduced lung capacity, headache, vomiting and internal bleeding. Because there is no known cure, there is a very slim chance of survival. So far, the government has only recorded 1 recovery in 10,000 cases. Those people never showed symptoms, and the conclusion was that as soon as someone shows symptoms, they only have hours left before it overcomes their immune system. At this moment, the country has recorded one million cases, so it may be that some of you sitting here have the virus already.'

I looked around carefully. I would have to proceed with caution. I hated that so many patriotic Americans clung so insistently to the idea of freedom of speech and movement; I was likely going to be villainised in their eyes after I spoke again. Perhaps their fear of the virus would dissuade them from disobeying authority.

'The government of the United States of America has agreed that because the Septosect organisation and its followers have such a large base here in Greenville, Utah, following the government's guidelines will be up to my discretion, since I am the face of our religious organisation. I want everyone gathered here today to know and understand the protocols that I will be putting in place under law.'

There was silence as I stopped speaking. I gritted my teeth. I had to be the voice of reason amongst a sea of trembling voices, whispered doubts and lurking fears. I would be the physical manifestation of the Lord. His messiah.

'There will be no leaving the village. Anyone seen going past the yew trees at the edge Ridge Road will be immediately expelled from Greenville. We will have no one come in. In this way, there will be no possible transaction of the virus. The good Lord gave us seeds to grow in times like this and all of our fresh food will be grown by ourselves. Storable food and other supplies will be ordered from a nearby factory that quarantines its products before they are sent out. All deliveries and parcels will go through the Septosect's protocols, which go directly through me, as I am your voice to our merciful God. You are allowed one delivery every three months, which will be approved by me before purchase. So that we can sustain our finances, we will be using the abandoned orchards at the edge of the village to grow fresh fruit to send to other villages in need. We must not forget charity in a time like this, as God expects us to work for our rewards and help those in need.

I know we are still finding out information from scientists as the days go on, but there is one shocking discovery I feel I must explain to you. A use of mobile phones and electronic devices has been correlated with a shorter window of incubation; that is, the radioactive waves seem to have some sort of effect on the virus, quickening its already deadly power. For your own safety, everyone must hand in their personal devices to this box here.' I pointed to a plastic bucket standing on the floor near the first row of seats. 'If you could start passing these along as soon as possible, that would be very helpful. Thank you. In the meantime, while I come around with another collection bucket, I would like to show you a news report on mobile phone usage.'

I stepped down from the pulpit and walked to pick up the other bucket, turning on the screen at the front of the hall as

I did so. Droning over my head, the blaring voice of a news presenter murmured about radiation exposure, the life span of viral proteins and 'substantial body of evidence' with reliable and trustworthy precision. I walked by the rows one by one, feeling control drip into my hands as one phone at a time was reluctantly handed over. No complaints, as I had previously thought there would be.

Down in the front row, I saw movement. Another of the children – Jude, if I remembered correctly. He was Halle's brother. He had slipped out of his chair and had run down the side of the town hall, tears streaming down his face as the sound of his small footsteps pattered softly on the stone floor. His sister stared concernedly in the direction he had run. I looked after him with a curious disappointment. At only 14 years old, he was the most high-risk of my mentoring group. I had been careful up until now always to present myself as a friend to him, even when his obstinate and ambitious nature presented itself as a challenge to me.

The news report ended abruptly, the screen going black. I put the bucket down and ascended into the pulpit for some final words.

'It is thought that these protocols will be in place for at least a year, maybe more. The Septosect won't lie to you: this isn't going to go away anytime soon. Stay strong, and have faith that the Lord has this all in his plan for us. Remember that He provided obstacles so that we could use them to work on our personal character and come together as a community.' Another infinitely benevolent smile. The pastor really was a pretentious man sometimes. 'I would like to see my youth group, please. Otherwise, I have no further news to give. You are all dismissed.'

I stepped down from the pulpit and looked around the hall, sighing. I had plans to renovate this place. It would be my temple of worship to the Lord. This was my chance to show others what it felt like to truly follow the divine Path of Faith.

The remaining children came forward as the rest of the congregation left, among them Ward, Halle, her sister Eden and Axel's daughter Daphne. They were the most important to me, along with Jude until he had run off. I, too, had plans for their futures.

'I hope you're all doing well, and that you're not too scared of what's going on. I know it must be very frightening, but you can trust me. I only want to keep you all safe, healthy and happy, as God would want it. I promise.' I knelt down so that I was eye-to-eye with them. 'Do you four mind helping me clear up the books at the side of the Hall?' I asked. Ward, Halle, Eden and Daphne nodded. I instructed the rest of the children to make sure all the seats were aligned and neatly organised.

We began to collect fallen prayer books from underneath the seats at the back: books that had fallen off shelves and hymn sheets that had been scattered near the back entrances.

I had only recently been instated as Septosect pastor for Greenville, an area where religious support had been dwindling in recent years. Extreme events had a funny way of creating solidarity – people wanted to be led and I was more than happy to be their shepherd and lead them to the Lord.

'After our mentoring session yesterday, do any of you remember what we talked about?'

'We talked about the Septosect and the creation of the Seven Pillars,' Halle said shortly.

'And can you tell me what those pillars are?'

'Honesty, Obedience, Love, Ambition, Faith, Loyalty, Knowledge. They were created in that order.'

'I don't remember,' Eden's small voice piped up. She looked at me with wide eyes. She was only seven, I reminded myself. Her head was so very empty, like a jelly mould that hadn't set.

'I'll remind you,' I said, curving my eyes upwards into a smile. 'When the Lord created the Heavens and the Earth, he took six days to do it. On the first day, he created humans and gave them a pillar of devotion with which to live by: Honesty. On each of the five following days, he instructed them with another pillar of devotion. Each pillar was a moral, a lesson to live by, which humans could interpret for themselves.

'You see, he wanted the humans to rise to his side and join him in Heaven as his lieutenants. However, he could only take the purest, most devoted of humans. And to test their devotion to him, he put them in the harsh and unfair conditions that we live in today.

'The Lord is not infinitely good. He is wise, and He knows that struggle leads to greatness. That is why he challenged his creations to learn and become better versions of themselves, by making them purposefully imperfect. However, on the seventh day, Lilith, who was the Lord's right-hand lieutenant at the time, was jealous of the care that the Lord was giving to his new creations. For she, too, had been created fallible. She loved the Lord and valued His wisdom above all His other traits. So, intending to help Him, she stole Knowledge and gave it to the humans, so that they too might grow wise like the Lord.

'When the Lord found out, he was furious, and banished Lilith to Hell, where she still resides today. An older, forgotten tale speaks of her falling in love with another human, but it isn't widely known. The Lord realised that some of his humans were becoming similar to Lilith; instead of staying on the true path of devotion, they deviated and strayed from the seven pillars. It seemed as if Love was not merely being expressed as devotion towards the Lord but was a connection between humans that caused them to dwell in sin and forget the seven pillars that the Lord had so benevolently provided for them. So, the Lord revealed to a select few humans, those who still spent their lives in devotion to Him, what would happen after death if they didn't follow the true path of devotion. They would be sent to Hell to join Lilith and burn forever,' I said. 'That is why we must all carry out the Lord's doing, so that we can remain the pure selves that we are born as and rise to His side after death.'

The four children looked apprehensive.

'Be excited!' I burst out. 'We are among the few who know these rules. We are a group above the rest of Earth's inhabitants, and we will be treated as such when we ascend.'

I shouldn't have been so loud. Pastors were meant to be calm and collected at all times. I struggled to don the face of serenity as I picked up another hymn book from the floor, carefully wiping down the cover.

Nora emerged from the back room, where she had been tidying up while I was speaking to the townsfolk. Just as the church submits leadership to the Lord, a wife should embody devotion and saintly purity. A cool shrug of disappointment slipped out before I could hold it in. I thought I had told her not to get blemished. It annoyed me that she hadn't listened. Now her porcelain features were ruined. I supposed her physical decline was inevitable; wrinkles were a part of every woman's descent from the pinnacle of their beauty. It wasn't just her looks that bothered me, but the martyr-like look of dejected sorrow that she wore as if it was an eternal fashion statement. Was this really the pastor's wife? I could hear the villagers murmuring to each other. I glanced at her coolly, pushing down on the inexplicable anger that arose whenever she moved too close. If she wanted to present herself so, it was her own fault that the other village women looked down on her, mocked her, thought her unworthy of her position as my wife. I wasn't sure whether I disagreed.

The hollow thud of a book landing on the floor made her flinch, and she quickly bent over to pick it up at the same time as Ward stepped forward too. I saw the flash in his impressionable eyes as she pulled up her sleeve and picked up the book, placing it carefully on the shelf.

I walked over to them with my ever-gracious smile plastered hard across my face. Although I had previously appreciated Nora's skin for its saintly expression of maternal care, it blemished easily. I couldn't let Ward see the stains on her crystalline complexion. It simply wouldn't paint the right portrait. I murmured an excuse to her. Delicately, gently, I placed my hand on the small of her back and walked her out of the town hall, her limp body silent by my side. Only her eyes still held that stricken look of a puppy that hadn't quite realised that its master didn't love it any more.

I could barely stand touching her; it was like touching glass. Outside on the damp grass, I removed her from my arm.

'Please tell Axel that I will be visiting his house tomorrow.'

She walked away silently, and I retreated back into the stony frigidity of the church.

A stained-glass window would look nice on the church's right-hand side, I mused as I stepped over the threshold.

CHAPTER 2

OBEDIENCE

I frowned at the rusty brown spots creeping over the corners of the delicate, wrought-iron frame of my window. My reflection, faint in the shadow of the sun, showed perfect blonde curls bouncing back up over my shoulders as I slowly dragged a hairbrush through them. The pathway in front of my house cut an imposing shape down our driveway.

I glanced at the dainty silver necklaces hanging quietly on a rack next to the window. I had chosen them myself, even though I preferred gold over silver. I had gathered that gold was simply too loud; at least, I had always been told that gold was too loud for a girl like me to wear. It would cast me in a poor light, my mother said. So would red nail polish, bright clothing, all black attire, hair tied too tightly and lipstick that was too bold. I took note of essentials like this but paid her no heed when it came to other matters.

Her expertise was in presentation, nothing else. For the past five years, I had learned from watching my father not to pay much attention to her opinion. I wanted to model myself after him, and finally gain a glance of recognition in return; hence, it simply wouldn't do for me to engage in petty conversations with her about different shades of colour that were appropriate for me to wear. I never disregarded my appearance, especially given how my father took pride in our presentability; I was sure always to do our family name justice. As the women of the family, we were expected to put our best face forward to make sure that the Daumer reputation was pristine amongst the Septosect seniors who might tap Father for future positions. I had never actually seen these seniors, though. It was mostly just Greenville townsfolk that I interacted with, although that was always accompanied with a sense of trepidation. It just didn't seem natural for me to spend time with them – it was as if we were on two different paths and there was no bridging the gap between us. I couldn't indulge in their menial everyday worries about trivial things; my family and I had a higher purpose. They spent their time gardening; we spent ours planning our final ascension to Heaven. My father reckoned that the Lord had sent this virus as a way to separate the chosen ones from the rest. With death around the corner at all times, who would carve the way forward for others who had earned a chosen path through devotion under the name of the Lord?

Thus, brushing my hair was important. Crucial, even.

I was absorbed in the task, admiring the delicate shape of my face and the perfect way my curls framed around it. I gave a small smile into the mirror. Was this the same smile that others saw me wear? Was this a smile my father would approve of?

I set the hairbrush down carefully, placing it next to the row of jewellery on the vanity rack. I watched the movement critically. Again, I asked myself what my father would think of the way I looked at this moment. Would he think me a pretty ornament, or would he notice my desire to join him in his work through the impatient movement I made? I must make a note to move my hands more slowly, more gracefully, if I ever hoped to meet his standards and surpass them.

There was a tentative knock at the door. A head bent round the frame as I twisted to see who it was. Just my mother.

'Good morning, my darling.' She looked me up and down and smiled. 'You look beautiful today.'

I brushed off the compliment with a shrug. She said it every morning, rendering its meaning useless. It wouldn't have mattered how many times she said it, though; every word out of her mouth was dull, pretty, lifeless.

'Your father wants to see you in his study.'

I jumped out of my chair and strode towards the door. *Slow down*, I reminded myself. *This isn't how a lady would walk.* I had been taller than my mother for a while now and stepping past her in the door frame made her body seem frail and thin next to mine. She hadn't been eating well but I couldn't bring myself to ask her about it. I had important things to be doing. 'Do you think navy would perhaps be a more flattering colour?' she asked me hesitantly, gesturing to her dress.

'Sure,' I said and moved down the corridor without looking back. I was already miles ahead of her and her half-attempt to bring me closer only made me want to pull further apart. If there was one thing I knew, it was that I didn't want to be like her.

The grand mahogany door was cool underneath my

knuckles. I steadied myself and knocked once. Twice. Three times. Decisive knocks but not too decisive. Not too weak either. They gave the right impression, I thought with satisfaction.

A raspy voice finally called for me to enter. I slowly swung the wooden door forwards and stepped into my father's study.

He was hunched over his desk, peering closely at a document that was illuminated by the reading light pointed towards it. His back was stiffly curved, wooden almost. I thought it proud; it was an honour to have a back so bent from the importance of one's research. I moved further towards the desk, tentative. He glanced towards me and I rose on my feet, drawing myself up. His irises seemed to spear through the rest of his eye, bloodshot from long hours spent pouring over documents. I knew it was critical work, the most critical work in the village. My father was the purest in faith, the most devoted. He completed prestigious projects for Harrison. I was proud to be his daughter. He beckoned me forward. 'Take these. I need Harrison to read this report.'

I nodded eagerly as he started muttering to himself once more, reaching for a pile of books by his side and flipping open the cover of the one on the top. He placed a few rolled up sheets at the front of his desk.

'Is there anything else I can help with?'

A single glance away from the book. 'If there is, I will tell you. Tell your mother not to disturb me for the rest of the day. We are approaching the end, and I must not be drawn away by the distractions of domestic life,' he said with his eyes ablaze in a glowing black.

If my father said it, then it was so. I prided myself on that fact.
'Of course. I'm sorry to disturb your work by asking.'

I might as well have been the breeze coming in from the open window. He was consumed once more. I reached across and tentatively took the papers from the desk. They felt important in my hands and I fumbled with them as I tucked them under my arm. A sheet wrapped inside started to slip and fell to the floor before I could catch it.

Another glance in my direction. Even as he was looking at me, I felt him turn away. He didn't have to say it; I already knew. I turned away and quietly left the study, papers still clutched in hand.

My mother was in the kitchen arranging a display of tiny pastries and fruits. The sweet scent of cherry oozed from the freshly baked treats. My mouth watered. I knew that the hard days of autumn's shift into winter would affect the village. Not us, never us: the Daumers simply didn't *do* hardship.

I walked past her, ignoring her faint call of goodbye as I grabbed my coat and stepped out through the side door. The leaves underfoot were mushy and wet as I tromped away from my house towards the church in the centre of the village. I was important, I reminded myself. It was ridiculous to be envious of pieces of paper.

I glanced down at them and my eyes narrowed. The first paper was a letter. 'Re: INNOCULATIONS', the subject read. My eyes dared not trespass any further down the page, and I stuffed it back under my arm.

The warm air from the chapel brushed against my cool skin

as I entered through the front door, making sure to slam it behind me. I hurried up the stone steps and towards the pulpit, where Professor Harrison was calmly knelt in prayer, hands clasped together. He looked the very image of devout worship; his brows were furrowed in concentration and his body was still and unmoving.

Dr Harrison was the beating heart of truth and honesty in this village. You could practically see the golden light that seemed to circle around him in a strange arc of devotion when he spoke in church; I would always be riveted to the spot, awed by his boundless authority and passion. I had believed every word he said. Who wouldn't, after such golden apples fell from his lips? Each one was a succulent promise waiting to be bitten into.

I admired the grandeur of the stained-glass windows to either side, depicting the Seven Pillars and the cherubs who gathered around each one, tossing freshly picked flowers onto the top of each of the pillars. I walked over to the statue of the Lord that resided calmly at the front of the church, muttering my affirmation under my breath.

'Dear Heavenly Father, we stand in envy and awe of your infinite wisdom and guidance of us here on Earth. May we all adhere to the Seven Pillars of devotion to maintain our faith: Honesty. Obedience. Love. Ambition. Faith. Loyalty. Knowledge. May your light guide us away from damnation and show us the purest ways to act in your image.'

Satisfied with the pious tone of my voice, I rose and stepped away from the statue. At the sound of my dainty footsteps, Harrison opened his eyes and turned towards me, his eyes lighting up in delight when he saw the papers I carried in my arm. That look of anticipation made my heart feel full enough to burst. In it was every aspiration I hoped to reach; in it was the confirmation that I was needed, that I was crucial, that I had a vital role to play in our ascension towards paradise.

I smiled widely as Doctor Harrison stepped towards me, greeting him with the same polite tone that I always extended towards my father's friends. He opened the papers and examined them carefully, brushing his beard with his hands as he read.

'Thank you, Daphne. Tell your father that I appreciate this. And thank you for coming all the way here when it's not your worship day. It must have been a cold walk.'

Could he tell from my flushed cheeks? I didn't want to appear messily put together; this was my time to shine as my father's messenger.

'Oh, it's no problem at all. Let me know if you need anything else,' I said. Was I being too eager? I was supposed to be calm, I reminded myself. Daumer women were calm and collected at all times.

He gestured politely that I was free to leave.

Stiffly, I marched down the chapel aisle. At the back, I noticed two heads bent together in silent prayer. The Marsh sisters, Halle and Eden. It must be their day of the week for an hour spent in spiritual reflection.

Harrison walked towards them. I looked closely at the younger sister's head. Why did her ringlets look so perfectly styled? Did she just wake up looking like that? A surge of jealousy that I quickly suppressed. It didn't matter. She was still irrelevant in the eyes of my father and the church. I didn't see *her* walking around carrying important letters to senior religious leaders. The other sister, Halle, looked up as Harrison approached. I certainly wasn't envious of *her*, with her dull face and limp hair.

'Good morning, both of you,' Harrison said quietly. 'I'm glad that you're here. May I ask where your brother and mother are?'

'I couldn't wake my mother this morning when we left to come here,' Halle explained. 'She works in the evenings into the night, and so she's often quite tired in the morning.'

'And your brother?'

'I'm not too sure where he is at the moment.'

I glanced with contempt at their heads once more as I exited the church. No brother or mother at their prayer sessions! It was shocking how undevout that family was, really. My father, my mother and I had never missed a single session, and sometimes we went multiple times a week. We were on a clear path to Heaven, whatever it took.

'That's the third week in a row without any prayer, affirmations or spiritual teachings. Tell your brother he is walking along a thin line. His faith is being neglected, and as a result he could receive a divine punishment. The Lord will not be pleased with this. I try my best to keep you all on the path of Faith, but it doesn't take much to stray.'

As the cold air hit my face, I couldn't help but think that no matter whether their brother came or not, that family just wasn't going to make it when the day of judgement came.

Them, at the side of the Lord? I simply couldn't imagine it. I knew it was a cruel thought, but in this desperate race to the top there wasn't any other conclusion to be drawn.

I stared at my potatoes in silence, watching the oil from my meat slowly extend over my plate. My father bit hard into a piece of bread, arm swivelling to reach for the plate of broccoli in the middle of the table. My mother's eyes were fixed downwards too.

The silence made me uncomfortable. I had never realised just how little conversation was held between the members of my family; such was the rush of urgent and busy matters that interaction wasn't a priority.

'How was your day, dear?'

A smooth tone one would adopt around a client; it practically ached with its signature, feigned cheeriness.

'Good, thank you.' My father paused. His eyes seemed strained.

All he talked about was the Lord; all he thought about, dreamed of, focused on, fixated around was his goal of ascension. I loved him for it and admired his passion and single-minded approach. It was what had earned him traction with Harrison in the first place. This struggle to diverge from the topic only proved his devotion, I insisted.

'Would you like more beans?' he asked. A further pause.

'I'm full, thank you.'

'I'll clear the plates,' I muttered, pushing my chair back and collecting up my cutlery. 'I delivered the message to Harrison this morning. He thanked me well for it. I was glad to be of use to you, Father. You know I'm always eager to assist you with anything you need and delivering messages could be a start.'

'Don't be ridiculous,' my father growled. 'Any old mule could deliver messages to and fro. Walking outside is a man's job; what I need from you both is to continue doing what you've always done. You represent this family, after all. I can't have you running around like an errand-boy. Today was a one-off emergency situation. Besides, you're better suited to being at home anyway, where you've always been.'

An immediate murmur of agreement from my mother. I wouldn't have expected anything different.

Any old mule could deliver messages. I stood woodenly, the half-dumped dinner plate heavy in my hands. It had always been a pretence, after all.

Smile. I smiled.

Nod. I nodded.

Make him happy. That's all that you want, isn't it?

Was it?

'Of course, Father.' My flat, lifeless tone was so very similar to my mother's. 'If you insist.'

CHAPTER 3

LOVE

Dust swept into the air, clouding the pale light that shone weakly through the blinds. The broom swept back and forth across the wooden boards, rising and lowering to touch the floor in soothing, repetitive motions. I watched it swing with unmoving eyes. My dirty hands, absorbed in the task, seemed to belong to another image of myself. This was a regular chore; perhaps among my favourites of all the chores I had to complete. Its soothing rhythmic nature allowed me a moment to escape without the guilt of actually taking a break.

'Halle, get me a glass of water,' rasped the voice behind me, followed by the sour sound of liquid sloshing into the toilet bowl. My mother groaned and I heard the slump of her body as she swung limply back onto the couch, exhausted from her efforts. Looking back at her briefly, I set my brush down carefully by the windowsill and dusted off my hands. Her eyes were closed in a pained expression, arm thrown over her face in a careless manner devoid of any delicacy. Her limbs seemed disjointed and awkward where they were illuminated by the faint light of the morning sun. Shade clouded the rest from my vision, but her body seemed to groan and heave silently alongside her, mourning what it had lost the night before and all the days before that. My mother had arrived back at home a few hours ago after a long night out on the other side of the village, which she frequented on a nightly basis. Of course, there was no question about my taking care of her; in the end I always did. Her feigned cheeriness always opened a swelling pit of guilt inside my stomach whenever resentment bloomed to the surface of my mind. I knew she understood herself too.

I stepped quietly out of the room.

The old tap had splotches of rust streaking bluntly up its side. I tried to admire the sharp audacity of the stains, but I couldn't find beauty anywhere in their ugly curvature. Was there not supposed to be some sort of consolation that I could find in nature, some poetic beauty that could sustain my hope while I batted on through my struggles? I liked the sun, but that was only because it made things clear, as clear as they could be to anyone who squinted to look. Other than that, I had seen the scenery out and around my house so frequently that none of it exhilarated me; I had already appreciated the curve of the leaves on the trees and the stark orange of their colour as they fell to the ground. I had already composed poems about the colour of the overcast sky, had already stared at peaceful stars gliding past my window at night imagining life on a distant planet, had already envisioned the soft crunch of snow as romantic and not as a soggy lump that froze my body.

There simply wasn't anything left of my house, of my situation, that could fuel me. Apart from Eden, that is. But I felt guilty using her to console myself; it felt like trespassing past the smooth white fence of the Daumer residence into their polished halls.

Since classes in the church had resumed again after the summer, I was given new subject matter with which to carve and sculpt in my mind. I could envisage my life as a girl like Daphne Daumer, twirling in pretty circles as she daintily reached for a glass from the shelf. Perhaps she would tilt her wrist – just so – as she twisted the tap, the stainless-steel glowing under her touch. The water would rush out in a giggle, almost sparkling in vibrance, as though her very presence had charmed it into the cup.

The ugly slosh of sputtering water, thin and pathetic, burned my ears as I reluctantly filled a glass. I reminded myself that Daphne Daumer had a heart too ugly to charm anything into a cup, least of all a soulless element like water.

When I walked back into my mother's bedroom, she was leaning unsteadily against the wall, breathing heavily. The faint cracks extending from the window darkened the paint slightly, spider-webbing around her fingers. *Cream is such an elegant colour*, she had told me years ago when we first moved into this house. *The perfect colour for a bedroom wall, don't you think?*

We had painted it ourselves, and she had insisted that we splurge on our very own paintbrushes – one for each of the five of us. Typical of her nature, I thought with a slight smile. She was always spending irresponsibly like that, as if she hadn't a care in the world.

I held out the glass of water silently. She stumbled towards me, the foul stink of her breath clogging my nostrils. Suddenly, she put her finger to my chin, her sharp nail drawing blood from the surface. Bloodshot eyes stared into mine as she roughly peered into my face. Her makeup was cakey, I observed with a slight disdain. She should try to blend it in better, instead of slapping it over every pore in a poor attempt at concealment.

'You're a pretty girl, you know that? Remind me of myself at your age. I still had that precious look of concern carved into my eyebrows when I was you. Of course, it's all gone now,' she slurred drunkenly, thrusting my chin away to lean heavily on the windowsill and grabbing the glass from my outstretched hand. Tipping her head back, she glugged down the water greedily. The ugly sound of her swallows disgusted the trivial, superficial part of my brain. Did she always have to drink in that way? I knew alcohol stripped back all subtlety but I couldn't help the irritation that formed under my skin.

Behind her, the blankets shifted as the lump beneath them started to take form. I needed to get whoever she had brought back out of the house immediately. Often after a night out, rowdy fights would ensue when my mother and her various partners both awoke and realised that the charming acquaintance they had met a few hours ago had transformed back into a rudimentary creature overnight. I disliked kicking them out myself, though. Most of the time the men she came back with weren't the type to take no for an answer and thought that a house inhabited by only women was the perfect pickings for a man looking for easy satisfaction. My mother had always prevented things from getting that bad, however. She was good at coaxing people to do what she wanted, too – something about the helpless gleam she carried in her eyes made men feel needed and important when she asked them to do favours for her.

'Did you manage to make that deal you were talking about making yesterday?' I asked with feigned brightness. I sensed what she was about to say before she even said it.

'Oh Halle, darling. I tried so hard to do it, I really did. I ended up getting scammed – old ass said that he wanted double, and of course I wasn't going to take that. Unfortunately, things got a little heated.' She chuckled in a forced manner. 'I barely got away in time, which is when I ran into this pleasant chap over here.' She motioned aimlessly towards the man still sprawled on the mattress. 'Helped me out of a right pickle, he did. Thought I should get to know him better, so I invited him round. He says he's got a man outside of town who can help us get cash quick.'

I raised my eyebrows. 'Outside of town?'

'Yeah, a real trusty source. He says there's money to be made in Salt Lake City and wants a little starting cash to invest. He's got an eye for up-and-coming businesses, apparently.'

It was almost painful how much she reminded me of Eden sometimes. They shared a naive but persistent optimism that kept us going but kept us behind. Ma with her business deals and Eden with her illness ensured that we would never escape this trap. The hopelessness of the situation, the knowledge that we were all likely to die of this virus, kept me ambivalent.

'I'm not so sure, Ma. You said this last month, too. I only have so much saved and, if we're not sure whether the investment will work out, I don't think we should risk it. Plus, I don't know how reliable this guy is.' I gestured at the man. I had never seen someone who seemed further from the definition of reliable.

In the shed planted in the cold grass behind our house, I watched my breath cloud the air gently as I heaved a box down from a cobweb-covered shelf. By my side, my sister seemed no more than an apparition. I tried to keep her inside as much as I could, but today she had insisted on helping me. She was already twelve, but her lungs were so weak that it was impossible for her to spend any length of time in harsh conditions. She fell sick frequently and I felt a constant seizing of my heart whenever she emerged from her room complaining that she didn't feel so good. Every winter was a constant risk of something worse happening. I didn't like to think about it. I had even asked Dr Harrison if Eden could skip our mentoring sessions but he refused, under the premise that the Lord wouldn't tolerate her straying too far from his wise and caring sight. Nowadays, the words *Harrison* and *the Lord* seemed awfully interchangeable.

A seizing cough choked its way out of Eden's throat.

I set my cardboard box down and looked, worriedly, over at her. The light cut the shape of her face in a haunting glow, her pale dress highlighting her flushed cheeks and wide eyes. For a minute, a strange feeling of pain passed over my heart. She reminded me of the sun sometimes, with the way she looked at me, so filled with the raw hope of change, despite nothing having changed in the five years since we had been shut off from the rest of Utah. Our little island of Greenville had been the centre of so much of her memory, yet she seemed to ignore the struggles I bore, that my mother bore, that she bore herself. It was always, *wouldn't it be nice if* and *I can't wait until.* Sometimes I wondered if she really was blind to the hopelessness of the situation or whether she chose simply to ignore it. Her bare innocence was almost comforting sometimes and excruciatingly exhausting at others.

'Are you alright?'

She nodded faintly. 'I haven't been able to stop it all day, and I don't know what to do.'

I knew what Ma would do if she found out. 'I'm not sure either. Hold it in?' I suggested helplessly. Uselessly. Her hands were shaking. I hesitated. 'Please don't tell Ma.'

'I won't,' she whispered. She wasn't stupid and she certainly didn't want to be taken to the Infirmary where Nora Harrison guarded over all the sick townspeople with silent, watchful eyes. It would mean immediate ostracism if Greenville suspected that Eden had the virus, and it would be impossible for Ma to attempt deals outside the village. The few vegetables we grew to help the village would be unacceptable food for others and that would mean we wouldn't be able to rely on this small source of cash any more.

I picked at the rice and beans in front of me. Ma was shoving down the food on her plate with a vigour that pricked my anger. I couldn't help but think that her only contribution to the household today was to bring home an extra mouth to feed and to gamble away what little money we had on his fly-by-night business ideas. She was going out again later tonight. I had reluctantly handed over to her a small wad of spare cash that I had bundled together from what we had left. I kept all my savings tucked away in a small nook behind the sink in the bathroom I shared with Eden. I had only told Jude where I kept my stash in case I caught the virus and my sister and mother were left without any money to support them. I wasn't sure what Jude would do if he was forced to return home to take care of them in my absence. He was practically a ghost around our house; all of his time was spent with his cronies on the other side of the village, where my mother visited during the night. Such was life, where we anticipated that death could swoop in at any time and pluck us out of our existence, robbing us of the journey that could have been or relieving us of our misery. Nowadays, I couldn't even rely on myself to support my family. I already knew painfully well what consequences the virus had on a body once it took hold. My father had contracted heart disease just before Greenville was isolated; he had died painfully, a few days into the lockdown. Although it was a shock for the first few months, Ma said she'd be better off without the arguing and the pretence that he was actually bringing in any money from the garage. At least, that was what she pretended.

A burst of breath came from my side. Eden was shaking, her shoulders moving in a laboured manner up and down as she coughed and coughed and coughed.

My mother and I looked at each other simultaneously.

'Halle, go and fetch Dr Harrison,' Ma said quietly. 'I need to get ready. I haven't curled my hair yet and my lipstick's a mess.'

I got up from the table, guiding Eden into the living room.

She lay, limp and pallid, on the musty couch in the centre of the room. Her forehead glistened. I clenched my lips together. I knew perfectly well what these symptoms were.

I turned away without another word and walked towards the front door. What could I do except follow my mother's orders? Sometimes the large coat hanging on the hook opposite the door, one that I dusted religiously, seemed to inflate with a dark fury when she passed by it. She was too wrapped up in her own world to notice, of course.

The symbol of the Septosect was faded, and the paint worn, on the wall next to the door. Beneath it lay a stand with the sacred text flipped open onto a page I hadn't turned it to. I rarely used the book for guidance or prayer; it was mostly my sister who followed it, and my mother used it to look up references to impress Dr Harrison with when he made his weekly visits around each of the houses. I had watched her flounce around him, with a passive smile stuck on my face.

When the lockdown was first introduced, I had touched the book each time I passed out through the door in hope and desperate expectation that some god, residing high and out of sight, was watching with a pleased smile. It was customary to place your hand on the book and say your affirmations before you crossed your own threshold, as a sign that you would carry the Lord with you whenever you ventured out into the world, past the safety of your own residence. Nowadays, I preferred not to think about the Lord whenever I could help it. I certainly understood that if He was real, He wasn't benevolent. Not by a long shot.

An hour later, Dr Harrison stood in our front room as Eden lay breathing raggedly, a strange look upon her face. It was dark outside now, and the only source of light was from the yellow lantern Harrison held in his hand. His clinical mask was stretched tight over his face, his dark eyes serious and sombre above it. I was glad I couldn't see his mouth; I had always hated his smile.

My dislike had started five years ago, from the very first Greenville meeting when lockdown had been established. The doctor had been talking about the impact of radio waves on our health, and I had been forced to hand in the very first phone I had been recently gifted by my father.

Radio waves? My limited scientific education at the small school in the village hadn't prepared me for this situation. I supposed Harrison must be right – he was a doctor, after all. Reluctantly, I dropped my sparkly flip phone in the grey bucket, hating the plastic clack as it dropped onto the top of the pile, my hand feeling empty and cold without it. I crossed my arms uncomfortably as the doctor moved on, smiling faintly at me as he breezed past. It was a smile of reassurance, but it dripped like slime.

That same smile was still there, just hidden. I was sure of it.

I could already see the peaceful resignation in Eden's face. She knew she was one of the weakest in the village; this wasn't a surprise. I wanted to shake her shoulders in anger.

'I'll take her to the infirmary. We'll see if her condition stabilises overnight. I brought a mask with me that she can wear until then.'

My mother nodded slowly. 'How serious is her condition at the moment?'

'I'm afraid I couldn't tell you. We still have so little information about how the virus works. But...' he hesitated. 'I'll let you say your goodbyes.' He stepped out of the room.

Goodbyes? Surely not *those* kinds of goodbyes?

My mother was already pressing into my sister's side, holding one of her small hands with both of hers. Her red nail varnish seemed jarring against Eden's pallid skin.

'Mama loves you so much, darling,' I heard her say. 'I'm sure you'll be alright – haven't you always been before? You're a strong girl.'

I saw for the first time, maybe, that Eden knew my mother as well as I did. She smiled wide beneath her mask, curving her eyes upwards, and hugged her mother tight.

'I know, Ma. You don't have to worry about me.'

'That's my good girl. You know I'm proud of you – proud of both of you girls.'

I could smell her perfume as she twisted her coarse locks to look at me. I didn't like it; it reminded me of unease and unfamiliar faces. It was always the scent she wore before going out. She glanced at her watch. Quarter to eight.

I thought of ripping it off her wrist and smashing it into the wall.

'Halle, hon, your hands are shaking. Come let me give you girls a hug.'

I received it stiffly and awkwardly, bending my arms like a wooden doll around her body. Eden was so light, it was like she wasn't even there. After a moment, Ma paused and we disentangled ourselves. She was silent for a minute before looking long and hard into each of our faces.

Murmured promises, thoughts of consolation, things we could all look forward to in the future when Eden returned safe and well.

Was that it? I thought. *I could have said those words to a stranger.*

My mother stood up and brushed off her jacket. 'I'll see you tomorrow, Eden. I'll come visit you in the Infirmary. I've really got to be going, otherwise this deal will be out the window!'

A nervous laugh, the sweeping of footsteps. The chirp of a 'Goodbye!' as she slipped out the door, past Dr Harrison and into the old car that was waiting for her on the dirt gravel. She remained blind, as always. I wondered whether her permanent state of half-sobriety, half-intoxication, clouded her vision of reality.

'I'll come and visit you,' I breathed. 'Tonight. In the infirmary. I'll sneak in so you don't have to be alone when…' I stopped. When. The inevitable when.

'I'm scared of Mrs Harrison,' Eden whispered to me quietly, grabbing my hand. 'When you had to leave the house for the day a few days ago – remember, she offered to take care of me while you were gone – she insisted that it was the perfect time for me to get my vaccine jab. It was for seasonal flu, she said. She took me to the Infirmary, and I *know* she used the same needle on another boy who already had the flu. I didn't want to say anything, and I thought she was the doctor's wife, so of course she knew what she was doing! But ever since then I haven't been feeling so well. The coughing only started today, when I couldn't hide it any more. I thought it would get better like all my other illnesses, but I still feel just as bad.'

Flu jab.

Dr Harrison's face appeared around the doorframe before I could reply.

'It's best if I take her now,' he said gently. 'I don't want you to have increased exposure and spread it to others. I know it's only spread mucosally, but it's extremely high risk if you do end up catching it. You know the drill.'

I forced out a nod and watched as he helped her stand, placing her hands securely in his gloved ones. The lantern he held swayed. He spared me only a glance before he strode out of the door, her small feet pattering behind him. The slam of the door shook the hallway.

Then I was left alone in the dusty living room, staring once more at the cracks on the wall.

Was I really the type to break into a building in the middle of the night? It was my final heroic goodbye to my sister; I was sure the Lord would excuse me this one time. The window of the infirmary, bordering the faintly lit room, was unlocked. An omen? Whatever the case, I chose to take it so. As I cracked it open, I could see the shadow of a hospital bed in the corner of the darkness. Laboured breathing. Breathing in shudders and stopping. Then breathing again. The sickly smell of illness. I was alarmed; had the end come so soon? I knew she was naturally weak, but I had hoped that she could hold out at least a little longer. Maybe just enough time for Ma to see her one more time. I didn't want Ma to disappoint Eden, but I realised it would be more for my sake than Eden's if Ma got to give her a proper send-off.

Someone sat up in the darkness.

I whispered hurriedly that it was me, and my voice was received with a soft cry. I knelt over the bed, able to make out the shape of my sister's face from the light from the cloudless night and from the faint illumination the door facing the corridor provided.

I sat in silence next to her, each breath of hers an ebb and flow of my anxiety. I would be there with her as long as I could.

My fingers tapped on the cold floor.

After a while, she seemed to muster the energy to speak.

'I'm finally going to see Him,' she said breathlessly. Something in her voice seemed forced. 'I think it will be beautiful up there.'

'Yeah,' I said lamely. I couldn't bring myself to respond in the way that I knew she wanted to, no matter how much I desired to reassure her.

Her long, sad face was outlined in the moonlight. I saw the curve of her cheeks, the soft bend of her nose, the point of her chin.

Sudden footsteps from the dimly lit corridor. Panic fluttered in my stomach. Was this going to be it? I clung onto Eden's hand for a desperate moment. I could think of nothing to say; no poetic last words came forth from my mind. All I could think of was the same phrase that every family said to each other.

'Love you,' I whispered.

'Love you, too.'

'Yeah.' I felt as shallow as my mother.

A quiet mumble barely heard over the whistle of the late-night wind.

'See you soon.'

I stepped quietly up to the window. A soft splash sounded as I jumped onto the paved path, puddle water spraying onto my leg. I crouched beneath the Infirmary wall, eyes on the ground.

I only heard a soft exclamation as the footsteps walked up to the bed and noticed the open window blowing frigid air into the room.

Then, a solid clang as it was closed shut, and the grating sound of a key twisting into a lock.

CHAPTER 4

AMBITION

The after-party for Eden's funeral was crowded and loud with the sounds of dozens of people muttering and murmuring to each other. Cheap plates and old cutlery were used to hand out snacks and soft drinks to the group of townsfolk who had come to mourn my sister's death. I accepted a piece of cake from an old lady who pressed it into my hand. It sat limply on top of its napkin as I held it by my side, the thin icing slowly dripping down the side of the spongy layer.

I was thirsty.

To my right, I could see Ward Turner with my sister, Ma wailing on his shoulder. I ducked behind a crowd to keep out of view. I wasn't sober enough to wield my usual patience in their direction, limited as it was. Ward Turner's presence made my eyes sting, and I wasn't interested in talking to Halle about Eden. Too many eyes on me, too much attention to how I was reacting. I didn't feel the soul-destroying sorrow, the endless loss, that I had heard others describe. Was I supposed to? I wouldn't feign it in front of her; my morals weren't that far gone.

I turned away. My throat felt so very dry and my thirst

couldn't be satiated by the weak lemonade being passed around. Walking out of the plastic white tent, I made for the edge of the soggy, trodden grass where an old car was waiting. Its sides were battered in from late nights and youths whizzing recklessly around the town of Greenville, attempting to delude themselves into thinking that excitement, progression, rebellion existed in a place like this.

I felt that time had frozen in this small area while the rest of the world had moved on around it. *I* had moved on around it. I didn't know what remained of life outside the town; all information was fed to us through the church like farmers stuffing their chicken with grain. I wanted what I had lost, but the memories of hopes past were too much for me to dwell upon without something more solid in my hands.

My arm reached forward, grasping for a bottle that wasn't there.

I sighed and got into the car, switching on the engine. I wasn't supposed to leave the funeral yet, I knew. *Eden would be rolling in her grave if she could see you now*, I imagined the townsfolk saying. She wouldn't be, though. She wouldn't have expected anything different from me at all.

I breathed out deeply, hands gripping the side of the sink. This was harder than I thought.

The wad of cash on the counter stared at me blankly. I was trembling, I realised. I needed a drink.

And I needed this money to keep going; to keep me fuelled. Hopefully, Halle wouldn't know I had taken it if she had entrusted its safety into the hands of several friends. I did care about her. I did. But this money was being hoarded in the hope of leaving this infected town someday, and that was a hope I hated. There was no leaving this town, especially for people like us. Even if we never contracted the virus at all. Better to sit back and enjoy trivial pleasures before our time was up and the virus spread through us all like a rash, as it inevitably would. I wanted to go down smiling, at least.

I grabbed the money and stuffed it in my pocket without any more hesitation. Then I exited the bathroom, taking care not to glance at myself in the mirror as I walked out.

The familiar welcome of the screen porch front door, ricocheting off its hinges, sounded as I pulled the car to the side of the road. Its rusty wrought iron design was now just a symbol of neglect for those who felt its repair was pricier than listening to it creak and bang at every entry. Jumping out onto the wet road, I slammed the car door closed behind me. I trudged towards the house I seemed to practically live in and stepped around sleeping inhabitants, passed out on the sofa. I had woken up early to go to the funeral and I wanted to go back to sleep. This evening I would inevitably wake up desperate for a drink, so I made sure the money was still in my pocket as I walked up the rickety stairs of the house and sat down. This place had been my fortress and hiding place for the last few years and it was for the first time, in the light of day, that I noticed that its walls were covered in peeling paint and scuff marks.

I pulled out the wad of cash, its weight burning like fire in my hands, and passed some over to a hand with tar-stained fingernails and a different tattoo on each finger.

He spat. 'Don't be late with the cash next time.'

I smiled weakly.

After dopey murmurs of intoxicated laughter from the gang of teens inside, I slumped into the seat of one of the chairs left lying around aimlessly in the front yard. In a few hours, I would hear the yells and exhilarated shouts coming from inside, music seeping out of the walls through cheap speakers. After so many years of coming to this same house, I had long grown bored with it. It was the same thing every night, after all. After a while, the exhilaration of adolescence had grown into languid weariness. Nowadays I preferred to spend my time outside, watching the local nightlife move in its familiar rhythms, with warm liquid trickling reassuringly down my throat.

I had been doing this for nearly five years. And still, the same bitterness arose when I spun down deeper and deeper into the grip of my drink. I was wasted and so was life; what the hell.

The church was so quiet with fear that you could actually hear the looks on people's faces. I was sandwiched between my two sisters, their small shoulders jutting into mine. Looking up at the tall man standing in the pulpit, I was terrified. I could feel the hot breath of my father on my neck from where he sat behind me with my mother.

Dr Harrison's voice was soft. Comforting. But I still felt my stomach drop when he switched on the screen and the sombre voice of a news presenter blared throughout the church. It was over. My chances were over. Hope floated away on the sound waves of the broadcaster.

I was smart, I knew that. I had the hopes of the teachers at my old elementary school riding on me that maybe, finally, this would be the kid that made it out of here and went on to live the life that people only dream of. Out of Greenville. Out of a broken home. I was university-bound, they said. And I had thought so too, until suddenly I was thrown into this mess of an emergency.

Doomsday was coming. According to Harrison, I had at most a few years left to live before the virus ended its dormant stage and started to take over. Then would be a few days of painful suffering, before most of us would eventually fall ill and not survive. The newscaster reported the country's latest death toll as if it were a weather report.

I stood up. I could feel the faint gaze of my family around me as I started running, running, running down the church aisle. I had to leave. This couldn't be it. This couldn't be all that would become of this life. I deserved more.

Now my only goal was to pack any gratification that the next decade could have brought into the days or years I might have left. That was all I cared about.

Two silhouettes in the darkness appeared, trudging towards me. As they got closer, I could make out their faces in the light of the nearby lamppost. My sister and Ward Turner.

Tired eyes turned to face me. I couldn't bear their weight.

'Jude. Where is the money you stole?'

'I didn't steal any money.'

'I know you did. You're the only person who knew where I kept it.'

The only person? It was strangely sad how she had trusted

me so much. I knew I was disappointing her every moment she looked at me, and yet I couldn't bring myself to apologise, not even this once.

'I'm telling you I didn't take the stupid money! Ma probably found it.'

Ward Turner was looking at me reproachfully. That boy was slimy with fake sincerity, and I hated him. Who was he to barge into our life and act as some saintly vision of charity? He was caught under the influence of Mr Harrison.

Halle seemed to give up. She had barely even started arguing, and already I could see she was tired of it.

'Where is Ma? She left the funeral just after you did.' She paused and looked down. 'Seems we can't even come together for Eden's sake.'

I shrugged. 'Dunno. She's usually somewhere over there.'

I gestured in front of me to the row of small shops and houses that lined the streets opposite us. This was the marketplace of the village, and also the place to go if you were trying to get something from out of town. Rowdy drunks were arguing, and I heard the faint smash of bottles cracking over a head. I had seen Ma around here many times, of course, but I never bothered to talk to her. She kept away from me too. Some instinct to avoid me, I supposed.

Halle paused, and I saw her face deliberate over her words. My vision was blurry with the warmth of the alcohol in my body, so her face looked fuzzy at the edges.

'I don't trust Dr Harrison or his wife. Eden told me that Nora Harrison was sharing her vaccination needle with another boy who was already ill. I need to tell Ma because I don't know what to do and I can't just leave it like this.'

I looked at Ward carefully. What was his stance? He was staring at the ground awkwardly, his eyebrows mashed together in a look of pity.

'What are you saying exactly? You're accusing Mrs Harrison of killing Eden?'

'I don't know. But I need to tell Ma at least.'

I motioned over to the opposite side of the road. 'I'm pretty sure she's there.'

As I squinted closer, I could just about make out the harsh blonde of curled hair and the swing of a cheap purse around a shoulder. Ma was latching onto the shoulder of an older man, clearly desperate for something, and pleading with him. I saw the man pull back in anger.

He shoved her off.

A slap to her face.

The silence afterwards as she looked at him.

When I turned back to look at Halle, I felt strangely embarrassed.

CHAPTER 5

FAITH

"Honesty. Love. Ambition. Loyalty. Obedience. Faith. Knowledge."

I murmured the words, their resonance against my lips a steady comfort. Opening my eyes, I knelt back in my chair and sighed. My elbows were numb from leaning on the table for so long. I hadn't noticed, so caught up in my reflection had I been. Numb elbows, a hungry stomach and limbs filled with the sensation of needles were all proof of my devotion to the Lord. He would know I was prepared to sacrifice my personal comfort for his sake and he would take that into consideration on Judgement Day. It was good to start the morning off with a prayer – it just felt right.

A head peeked around the door at the side of the room.

"I just wanted to let you know that Harrison has arrived. He says that he got the letters that you gave Daphne. He's waiting outside as I told him you were busy.

'You left him waiting outside?' I asked. 'All I ask of you is that you put a good face forward for the Daumer family; Greenville expects nothing less from its morally right citizens.'

'I'll show him in now.'

I stood up and walked around the front of the desk. 'This isn't what I want when we're so close to the end. The Lord has his plan in place, and soon I will ascend to His side. We must show respect for the Lord and his chosen men.'

'Okay, dear,' said Lisa with scepticism. *Okay, dear.* Lisa found it difficult to understand the landscape of things. Even now at a time of crisis. In the early days I was pleased she married me. I was a drifter without a job until I joined the Septosect and found the Lord. My faith gave me an escape from Greenville's mediocrity and my father's failed dealings that left us penniless. Of course, the inheritance from Lisa's father helped my escape as well but I had brought us into good standing in Greenville through my relationship with the Septosect. Now my only simple request was that she could try to be who I wanted her to be and support my religious ideas. Fortunately, Lisa's demure nature made it impossible for her to express much opinion, which helped me steer her in the right direction. Still, her voice was uncertain and weak and at this moment, such uncertainty underscored my fear that we would die, forgotten and inconsequential, when the virus eventually took hold.

'It is certain that our doomsday will come soon from the virus. These times are not for the faint-hearted. Only the believers of true faith will rise to sit eternally at the right hand of the Lord. I will be one of those people. I would suggest seeking forgiveness from the Lord himself for doubting in his divine plan. You seem as if you don't care at all. Now go on, show him in.'

Harrison's dark eyes bore into mine. He placed his fingers carefully on the desk in front of him. My desk.

'Axel, I'll be honest with you. You seem a little off these days. But admittedly, your ideas are flawless, as they usually are. This is no exception. I fear the village is losing faith in us after so long under government guidance. A little girl contracting the virus? It's a harsh reminder that residents need to stay inside the parameters of Greenville. We can't have people getting restless. Eden Marsh wasn't the angel people thought she was anyway – not growing up with a family like that.'

I looked at him. What had this got to do with the Lord? With my commitment and unquestioned patronage to his service?

'I'm glad you appreciated it,' I said stiffly. 'Vaccinations are easy to mix up and confuse if there aren't eyewitnesses. All in the name of the Lord, after all. But I'd really like to discuss our plan...'

A twist of golden hair out of the corner of my eye. I looked through the sliver of open door, but I could no longer see anything.

'What plan?'

'Converting Greenville to the belief of the Septosect,' I said fervently. 'The more members we have, the closer we are to Heaven.'

'Yes.' He looked strangely bored.

'I have never had any reason to walk in any other faith but that of the Septosect. It is a privilege to be a believer, knowing that my life sins will be forgiven and my weaknesses overcome. I pity the unfaithful who are not able to live by the Septosect's seven pillars; I am aware of the dangers of defection. I have always deferred my decisions to the Lord, given my trust in his rules for life. If disease strikes, the Lord will look after us. I pray every day and I go to the church as often as I can to answer the call of the Lord. But still, I hear a silence from him. I am sure you must have a deeper connection.'

'Indeed, the Septosect is flourishing under the guidance of pastors like me. The Lord has spoken his will through me and continues to do so. He told me it was our duty to keep these citizens here, instead of letting them go where the sins of the rest of the world can reach them.' He leaned forwards. 'Perhaps this requires some extra time and energy on your part. I would suggest visiting the church soon for some clarity.'

'Of course. Anything to gain the Lord's favour.'

The blank page was spiralling away from me. I was breathing shallowly, hands shaking as I held the document. Why was the air so warm? I needed to get out of this study.

I stood up abruptly, shoving my chair backwards, and stumbled across to the door. I wasn't feeling well. Was this some kind of punishment from the Lord? Some kind of payback for a sin I had committed? I wasn't a sinner; I had followed Harrison and the Lord's will from the moment the lockdown was implemented. I never questioned anything about my Septosect faith and I knew my rewards would come; I had sacrificed everything to reach it.

As if in response, an epiphany flashed through my mind

as if I were being spoken to from above: the church, with its stained-glass window and an apparition of Eden Marsh. A reminder from Harrison, or a divine message. It had to be divine. This was my chance to prove my devotion outside of Harrison's shadow.

I felt redeemed that the Lord had revealed himself to me. I was not forgotten by Him.

As I grabbed my jacket from its rack by the front door, a face appeared to my right to see whether I was all right. Daphne. I didn't even hear her concerned question before I darted out of the door and hurried myself down the driveway. I wasn't supposed to rush, but I didn't care. I had to get to the church.

The doors were open and I ran through them. It was eerily empty, and the light from the stained-glass window cast the worn chapel seats in a hazy yellow.

There, at the altar, stood the statue of the Lord, alone and devoid of Eden's ghost that had earlier teased my mind. His face was infinitely wise, infinitely calm, infinitely superior. I fell to his feet, feeling the faint prick of tears in my eyes. I considered the death that could be around the corner for me and for everyone here, and it fortified me to think that the Lord was my saviour. I kissed the statue's feet. The hard stone against my mouth grazed my skin. I heard the sound of a shadow shifting behind me. I knew Harrison guarded his relationship with the Lord above everyone else's and he protected his reputation for being Greenville's most pious. Surely, he would understand my need to be alone with the Lord at this moment. Slowly, my breath returned to normal and I calmed, raising myself into a sitting position. It was quiet. I looked down at the mess I had made: the faint bloodstain on the statue, my face smeared. Lisa and Daphne would wonder what had happened to me.

I rose to my feet and brushed down my jacket. My head still had not cleared; if anything, the pounding headache from running all the way here had only got worse. I put a hand to my head carefully, leaning against one of the pillars.

I should go back home, I thought. I needed to get myself together. Slowly, I began to walk down the aisle and, at last, through the large wooden doors. The cold smell of the autumn wind hit my face and I heard muffled voices coming from around the corner. I started, before turning to see who it was.

An old couple stood there on their way to pay respects to someone who had died years ago. They were old-timers in the village and had been here long before Harrison had steered the community towards the Lord. They were leaning against the precious stained-glass window, the one which I had helped Harrison commission. The window seemed to groan under the weight of their backs. Everything was surrounded in a hazy glow as I wobbled towards them. Why did my feet feel so light?

'Please go,' I rasped.

They looked at me, wrinkled faces bewildered.

'The Lord rewards those who believe and his house is refuge for those who fall in the footsteps of the Lord through the Septosect!'

They moved back, allowing me to recognise the man who last year had questioned the principles of lockdown at a community meeting. In his former life he had been a science teacher and he still wore the spiritless look of fact over faith. They had tainted my privacy with their unnecessary presence. How disrespectful of them to lean against a religious depiction.

I began wiping at the window desperately, swiping at it with my jacket sleeve. The stain must come off. The Lord couldn't see what had happened, else he wouldn't think Greenville the holy place I had spent so long trying to make it into!

'How could you?' I cried, whirling to face them. 'I could have you regret this, you know. The church of the Septosect is a powerful place. Where have you been for the past five years? Were you not aware that our doomsday is coming?'

I barely heard their mumbled response before I turned away, squinting my eyes in the light of the hazy sun. It was almost sunset. The world seemed airy and bright as I wobbled away from them. I felt a strange euphoria as I tipped my head back towards the sky.

'All in the name of the Lord,' I muttered as I walked off. 'My time is coming.'

CHAPTER 6
LOYALTY

The sound of water splashing into the sink drizzled faintly into my ears. I stared at the wall. The rustle of leaves outside cut over the faint sound of Harrison's laboured snoring, his dark form faintly visible from the dim light of the bathroom I was standing in.

I turned off the tap, still watching the harsh shape of his body under the blanket.; he would remain asleep for several more hours, until the sun came up I had to go downstairs to the infirmary; our house, to the left of the village, also served to give medical care for all of the town folks who fell ill.

To check on the patients, he said. It was my job as the village nurse and his wife.

Check meant several different things, although of course he was never present for those moments.

The white of the bed cover shifted slightly with each of his inhalations. I slipped past him, careful not to make too much sound. After five years living in Greenville, I had mastered the art of walking quietly in the early morning.

The stairs shook quietly with every tread. I stared into the darkness of the unlit house, shrinking into the comforting coolness of the wall beside me. It was just another day, another repeat of what had already happened. I had done it before, and I could do it again.

Still, I couldn't pause the overwhelming emotion that arose in my chest when I landed at the bottom of the stairs every morning. The infirmary was down the hall and then through the corridor on the right. Every day it was a struggle to reach it. Somehow, I had kept treading along the hall every day, step by step. Even when the man upstairs, still sleeping peacefully in his bed, retained his pearly glow. Every day I felt my mind become darker, felt the crush of guilt weighing on my shoulders. Was it all his fault? Was it my own, for not being able to deny him what he asked of me?

Patients had come and gone for years. Their lives – and deaths – had been a steady trickle of guilt onto my conscience. But not his hands – never his.

Even though I had only wanted to be the village nurse.

The hallway breathed sleepily as I made my way through it, still feeling the rushing of my heart in my chest, the thirsty squelch of its beating uncomfortably loud. Another turn, and then I would reach the infirmary entrance.

Step, I commanded myself.

I hadn't minded the things Harrison asked me to do at first. I had been so consumed by my love for him. A doctor, and well-renowned within the Septosect community. How could a man so devout, so saintly, ask me to do such things and be refused?

I hadn't enjoyed the feeling of plunging a needle into skin.

But I wanted to demonstrate my loyalty to my knowledge, and to Harrison, that vaccinations would be our only way to fight this disease and get Greenville back to normal. I had wondered why it felt so wrong when I knew it was right. He told me it was the Lord's plan, so how could I refuse? How could I ever refuse Harrison?

I had quietened long ago, though. It was only in the mornings that I felt this way, and it wasn't every single day. Just occasionally, right after a death or on the day of a person's injection.

A muffled thud shook the walls. I froze. Was it an intruder?

Edging along the corridor, I heard footsteps that followed the thud. The quiet undertones of one set seemed to be undercut by the loud tromp of another.

The infirmary office, I realised. They were in the office.

I took a breath and turned round the corridor corner, finally making it to the infirmary office steps. Just down this flight I could hear the faint whispers of hurried voices. The stairs were so familiar that I didn't need light to guide me down them. There were faint flashes from inside the room and I realised the intruders must be carrying torches. What could I use against them? I had no bat, no knife, no gun.

I avoided the creak on the fifth stair and pressed myself into the wall, peeping my head silently into the room. In the corner, I saw the window blown wide open, the linen curtains blowing gently under the winter moon. The air motion had set off a cascade of curtain-waving, the blue hospital type curtains on plastic rods, surrounding each patient, waving in unison across the room as if ceremonial dance. I often left the windows unlocked after I said goodnight to the patients who slept down the hall. No one would dare risk viral death to attempt robbery.

'There's nothing here,' I heard a frustrated voice hiss.

'Stop this, Halle. Please. I know it's been hard, but you can't blame Harrison for what happened to Eden.'

My eyes stared rigidly in front of me. Halle Marsh? Was Halle Marsh in my house? And she was looking for evidence. Evidence against Harrison. My husband.

I pursed my lips silently and looked down at the floor. My hand longed to reach round the wall and flick the switch to the large TV that sagged against the wall.

It had been my duty to follow the orders that Harrison gave me. My divine duty as his wife, as a nurse, as a follower of the Septosect. But I wanted the guilt to go – for the endless noise of trickling blood that rushed through my brain to cease and halt forever. This was my chance to reveal my sins. It wasn't Harrison they should be looking for evidence against, but me.

Slowly, surely, I inched my hand round the corner. Just one flick of a switch, and the truth would be revealed.

My fingers quivered.

I deserved to be exposed. I deserved to face the consequences of what I had done. I had known for a while that it wasn't the Septosect that drove me to obey Harrison's orders. It was the pain of ignoring them and the repercussions I faced if I disobeyed that I feared. But this was my chance for Harrison never to find out it was me.

I gripped the switch and firmly shifted it downwards.

As the light of the TV blared into the room, I turned away, melting once more into the darkness.

CHAPTER 7

KNOWLEDGE

My finger pricked as I picked my way through file after file, slicing my hand against them every so often in my hurried discomfort. This felt wrong. The light from my torch was too harsh, too revealing. This was not how I wanted to be spending my night, especially since it was Harrison's house we were breaking into. I wasn't sure what the rules of the Septosect were in terms of breaking and entering, and I certainly didn't want to find out. Halle had been the one to drag me here, after all. I hadn't been able to say no; my promise to Harrison was too strong in my mind.

The office was warm and cosy, the pale blue rug worn and stretched. Dark furniture lined the walls, and a large bookshelf rested adjacent to the window on the right-hand side. It seemed not like the office of one of the highest ranking Septosect officials but, instead, like a homely place to sit and spend long hours talking. Was this truly where Dr Harrison worked all the time?

Lockdown had only been announced a few weeks ago, and

I had been called to Dr Harrison's office to have a little chat about my progress in the mentoring programme that I was taking part in along with the other children. None of them had been asked to come, though.

'Ward Turner,' Harrison said, a smile crinkling the skin around his eyes as I stepped into the room nervously. 'I'm so glad we could have this chat. Please, sit down.'

I cautiously perched on one of the large armchairs sagging in the middle of the room. It was too comfortable not to sink further back into the chair after a moment. Harrison turned to his right and reached for a tray on which perched two mugs and a few small cookies. He handed me a mug and I cautiously accepted, reaching for a cookie on his instruction a moment later.

The cookie crunched deliciously into my mouth, and I savoured the chocolate pieces scattered within. From beyond the steady chewing I heard in my head, I heard Harrison ask me a question.

'Our mentoring programme has been going well, don't you think?'

I nodded furiously, mouth too full to give a proper reply. After a moment, I swallowed and took a slurp of the drink he had given me. It was hot chocolate, slightly watery, but I didn't mind.

'I think you've made great progress, Ward,' he said, watching my face as I drank. I wiped my mouth quickly.

'Thank you, sir.'

'It's because of your dedication and cooperation that I want to ask you something special.'

Dedication? Cooperation? Those sounded like important words to me. My chest puffed out and I carefully set my drink down on the floor. I looked at Harrison eagerly.

'I have a little issue that I would love your help with, Ward,' he continued. 'There's a couple of girls in our mentoring course – the Marsh family girls. Halle and Eden. Do you know them?'

I nodded vaguely. I didn't know them, but I would make sure to become acquainted with them soon. Harrison didn't need to know that, though.

'Well, they're a bit of a special case in this village. They've got a lot going on, and I would love it if you could provide special support to them. You know, be their friend, help them out, show them around this village. Treat them with kindness. They only moved here right before the lockdown. Can you do that, Ward?'

I straightened, looking him in the eye. My small body was filled with pride. Of course I would do it.

'Yes, sir!'

He chuckled. 'Don't worry about being so formal. You and me, we're friends now, all right? I'm counting on you to do this for me.'

Hence had followed years of periodical visits, each one longer than the last, when Harrison would bring me hot chocolate, and I would curl into the armchair in his office and we would talk. I had savoured those meetings for the way that he looked at me. Like he trusted me, and only me, with the information he was giving me. Like I was something special. And in turn, I too had confided to him my childish concerns and fears, which he would always quickly put to rest.

So, I had stuck by Halle's side for these past five years. She was all right, I supposed. A little annoying, but I put up with it for Harrison's sake. And I truly did feel bad for her for what had happened to Eden.

I wasn't sure whether he would agree with what I was doing, but how could I ignore his advice? I was treating Halle with kindness, after all. And I knew the desperate look in her eye was only going to heighten if I said no to this night-time break in, ridiculous as it was.

A flicker at the back of the room caught my attention. There was a small *click*, and then, suddenly, the bright light of a TV turning on blinded my eyes. I thought I saw the faint outline of a body moving in the darkness but, the next moment, the TV started to play and my attention moved to the screen.

The news presenter was dressed in red. Something about the serious curve of her cheeks seemed hauntingly familiar as she started to speak.

'Recently there has been a particularly bad outbreak on the south-west coast,' she said. Suddenly, the image switched to a man with a blue tie. He began to talk about death rates. Then there was another switch. This time it was a clip about the rate of infection.

Halle picked up the remote which was lying on the desk and switched the sound off. Her eyes were wide, staring at the screen, as I looked at her uneasily.

'It's stitched together, Ward. Jude, you see it too, don't you?'

'This feels wrong, Halle. We shouldn't be seeing this. It's not for us to know,' I said in a pained voice, ignoring what she just said.

'Ward, you don't understand. *Daphne Daumer* was practically begging me to listen to her after I left chapel the other day. She was waiting for me outside and told me it was important that I listen. She said she had seen something on a document her father Axel had asked her to give to Harrison. Guess what was on the document?' she asked wildly.

'What?'

'The name Eden Marsh, under the title "Vaccinations".'

I sighed and waved my hands irritably. 'So? That doesn't mean anything.'

Jude stood silently in the corner. I couldn't tell what he was thinking; his face was shrouded in the darkness of the room.

'Eden told me before she died that Nora Harrison shared her needle with a boy who was already ill. How can you say that it doesn't mean anything?'

'Halle, I think you're getting a bit ahead of...'

'That's not all. Daphne also told me that she overheard Dr Harrison and Axel Daumer talking about how Eden's death was working well to stir up fear in the village. Don't forget, this is Daphne Daumer we're talking about – the girl who before yesterday couldn't bear to give me more than a sideways glance! She was so insistent that I know, that I thought she had come down with something. How can you just dismiss this?'

'Because you're *looking* for ways to find Harrison guilty, Halle,' I said angrily. 'You're not going about this in a logical way. I know this is hard for you to deal with and death isn't easy to handle. We *all* know. Everyone in this village has lost someone – and now you've lost another. You can't rationalise it. Sometimes death is just death. There isn't a reason behind it, there isn't some revenge you can exact, there isn't anything in the whole world that can explain why someone was taken from you. I understand. Losing my grandfather last year was extremely difficult to cope with. So, please, just let Eden rest. She's with the Lord now. You should respect that.'

'Look around you, Ward! There's nothing *here*. Where is the medical equipment that Harrison asked the town to contribute towards buying? Where are the gloves, the coats, the protection, the medicine? Do you see any?'

I looked around. Apart from the desk, computer, files and TV in the corner, there was nothing. Yet, I knew it was a mistake. We were searching in the wrong place. The equipment might be in the patients' room.

'This isn't some big coincidence,' Halle whispered fervently. 'This isn't something you can just explain away. We have to *do* something about this.' 'And how are we going to explain that we broke into a house in the middle of the night – Harrison's house, no less – and found out that a few pieces of equipment were missing and there were some clipped news reels on the TV? What are you going to say then, Halle? Who are you even going to tell?' She was silent, looking at me reproachfully in the light of my torch. Her lips pursed. 'Let's just go,' I said tiredly. 'Please, I've had enough.'

'No. I'm not going. This is too important.'

I glared at her, stepping forward and grabbing her by the jacket. 'Move, *now*. This has gone way too far. Harrison hasn't done anything wrong. He's been here for you all these years.

You in particular. How dare you turn your back on the kindness he's shown you? I'm not staying here a moment longer, and I'm not letting you meddle either.' I pulled her in the direction of the open window, her hands tugging against mine to let her go. I refused, and practically shoved her out of the window and onto the concrete below. I was shaking with anger. How could she question Harrison in such a way? The man who had shared his secrets with me, who had fed me hot chocolate, who had made me feel like I was valued for the first time in my life – how could she think so badly of him? I jumped outside too and heard the thud as Jude landed behind me. I rounded on Halle once more.

'Someone as devout as Harrison would never do anything to hurt people in this village. Greenville is under government jurisdiction anyway – someone would know if there was any foul play.'

'I'm sorry, Ward. I'm not going to continue living this life under his lies.'

'Do you know why we are friends? Why I approached you in the first place five years ago?' I asked her viciously. She fell silent. 'It was because Harrison asked me to. He asked me to treat you kindly, and I have ever since. Why else do you think I would be friends with a bore like you! And yet, still you seem to think that Harrison is out to get you, when he has shown you nothing but kindness.'

There was a silence in the cold air around us. I felt bad. I shouldn't have called her a bore.

She didn't seem to be reacting to it though.

'Well,' she said quietly. 'I'm glad you got it off your chest. I'll tell you why I decided to accept your friendship all those years ago. Would you like to know?' she said softly.

I said nothing.

'It was because I looked at you – we all looked at you – and saw in you what Harrison wanted for this town and its children. You had such a strong faith in the Septosect. In the Lord. In Heaven. You made me believe, even if it was only briefly, that we were truly going to go there. You were the only person I had ever come across who ever seemed to truly, really, believe Harrison's words. And I wanted so badly to believe them too that I looked to you to help me. I don't think I believe any more, Ward. I think you might be the only one who does.'

Jude was watching me closely. I could see the strange glint of pity in his eyes. At once, I felt a strange overwhelming sensation in my mind. Was it frustration? Humiliation? Anger? They didn't understand. I realised that they probably never would.

'I'm leaving,' Halle said quietly. 'I'm leaving this village. There's nothing keeping me here any more. And I'm not coming back, either. You won't have to worry about that. All I ask is that you don't say anything to anyone about breaking into Harrison's house. I promise I won't disturb your peace if you don't want me to. I want my sister's death to be brought justice, though. But I suppose in some ways you're right. Even if Harrison was found guilty, it wouldn't bring her back. So, that's all I ask.'

Her tone was soft. Settled. I refused to meet her eyes, instead keeping my eyes on the ground. My instincts urged me to go against everything she had said, to run straight to Harrison and tell him what she had told me.

'I won't.' The words were curt. They cut my tongue as they left my throat. I was betraying my faith, I knew. Would I go to Hell for this, or was it a good decision to make?

A look of surprise from Jude at my agreement. I bristled, but his lanky form was already walking away disjointedly, loping back to his side of the village. Not even a word of acknowledgement towards his sister. I didn't think he had said a word the entire time we had been here. There would be no goodbyes between them either, I assumed. It didn't seem as if Halle noticed or cared.

'Thank you,' she said. I said nothing in reply.

She started walking slowly in the opposite direction from her brother. I knew this might be the last time I ever saw her, but I didn't know what to say. Was there anything?

She didn't seem to think there was, so I trudged awkwardly away, glancing back every so often to watch her silhouette fade slowly into the darkness.

I began to retrace the well-worn path towards my house in the darkness. It should be all over now, shouldn't it? She would leave, and Greenville would live once more undisturbed. It would all be as I wanted.

A while later, I softly let the clack of my front door slide shut. The noise was haunting.

Everything was fine, I thought, staring into my dark living room.

So why, then, did I feel so uneasy?

Anna Pattle is a seventeen-year-old student at Wycombe Abbey School. She found the inspiration for this book while being locked down in London for the 2020 COVID-19 pandemic. This is her second novel, the first being *Sardaron*, a fantasy fiction novel which was published in 2018. Anna enjoys creative writing in her free time and this short book was the culmination of thoughts about how an isolated community might respond to the threat of illness and loss of freedom. Anna aims for this book to provoke thought about global responses to COVID-19.